Good Night, Princess!

By Andrea Posner-Sanchez

Illustrated by Francesco Legramandi and Gabriella Matta

Random House 🏠 New York

ISBN: 978-0-7364-2851-4

www.randomhouse.com/kids

MANUFACTURED IN MALAYSIA

10 9

It is nighttime in the kingdom. Everyone will be going to sleep soon. What do princesses do to get ready for bed?

Belle always reads a bedtime story before turning out the light and going to sleep.

Snow White gives a good-night
kiss to all her friends.

Rapunzel brushes her long, long hair every night. It takes a long, long time.

Down below the waves, the Little Mermaid prepares for bed. Ariel sleeps in a giant clamshell.

Tiana listens to a jazzy lullaby
before she falls asleep.

Cinderella likes to have a glass of milk and a
snack before brushing her teeth and going to bed.

Aurora always takes a bubble bath
before putting on her nightgown.

Good night, princesses everywhere!